Flowers C

Curtain

Sandeman (Jim) Craik

Dedication

THANK YOU…

* Dianne, who has been the star in the sky of my life, always there, bright and strong.

* my friends who have inspired me, given shoulders when I cried, wisdom when I wondered, listened to me, always wrapped me in kindness.

* my families for their love and for the feelings of pride at their success.

* Colin who always encouraged me, the Crown Prince of Procrastinatia, to stand up and speak, and to sit down and write and paint.

Contents

Page Blank Intentionally

Flowers on a Curtain

50 years ago, and 5000 miles away I wrote a poem ....

FLOWERS ON A CURTAIN
They blow in the wind. They fade in the sun.
They even close at night.
But they are as dead as words in a letter.

Words though in a letter, in a book, on a page, on a screen, I believe, do come to life when they are read, when they are spoken.
So, here are some poems from three of the curtains of my life … Flowers, Un Melange, & Two Little Ducks. Open them.
Read them. Enjoy my words. Give them colour, say them out loud, sing them, help them to blow in the wind.
Smile too occasionally, perhaps.

Sandeman, aka Jim, Craik
Los Angeles
December 2023

BLUE BALLOON

I was blowing up balloons
many years ago, for Isabel's birthday party.
As I struggled to tie the knot, one escaped
and rocketed across the room
zigzagging, making a sound like a loud fart.

Narrowly missing Grandma, it hit the wall
next to the David Hockney painting of Mulholland Drive,
and slid down, finishing up in a small pool
of blue rubber behind the couch.
The children laughed so loud; the dog barked.

Now, in this empty room, the droplets,
the particles of the memory of that laughter
have infected me, leaving me
alone but with love and hope.

A THURSDAY MORNING IN SPRING

Blossoms on the apricot trees.
Sweet peas next to the bird bath
climbing their canes, completely covered with red flowers.
Morning sun, still low; half my garden dark with the shadow
of the lawyer-next-door's tall trees.
Two hummingbirds hover, one darts away,
they play chase like balloons escaping
from a children's party.

The five palm trees down the hill
on the street below are still.
No breeze. No movement
except a hawk circling, crying like a locked-out cat,
and the cars and trucks trickling
down the Hollywood Freeway,
towards Downtown where the skyscrapers
are still dark against the pale sky, waiting
for the sun to paint their towers fresh bright shining silver.

I must write to my grandchildren and my friends,
I am reminded. They are dark like those buildings,
waiting for words from me,
waiting to show me, in return, their bright lives.
I must write.

HOPE

These days my garden
has been bright with butterflies.
I love their colours
and the way they take my attention
to the different flowers
that would have been unnoticed,
bringing them, one by one, on to the runway
of a botanical fashion show.

I watch a yellow monarch fluttering, gliding,
and I remember the gentle tickle
of its soft wings when I caught one once
and held it carefully in my cupped hands,
a tickle as tiny as a kiss from a stranger,
lips cold as a full moon.

****

*To some Native American tribes, the yellow butterfly brings
guidance and is a sign of hope.
A yellow butterfly represents joy and creativity.*

WHY?

I used to love tuna,
ate it all the time,
but recently I have found
it just doesn't tickle my palate
like it used to.

SAIL, A FATHER'S SONG

You left home today, Miss Amy Rose,
on your voyage of discovery.
From the high cliffs of my predictably unexciting life
I watched your sails fill with the winds of knowledge.
I waved until your ship sank out of sight
over the horizon up Highway 5 North,
taking you to your new world
where your every day will be a tomorrow.
I remember in the legend of Ariadne and Theseus
she gave him a sword and a ball of thread.
We have given you the sword:
enthusiasm, to look forward, to always see the light,
commitment, the strength to keep going,
imagination, to exaggerate, illustrate, elaborate,
wisdom, to remember and use what you have seen,
vision, to think of what is beyond the sunset,
education, to enjoy the poetry, music, wonders of the world,
and *experience,* to allow you to travel alone but safe.
We have made your sword as strong as love,
as sharp as truth, and as bright as your future.
I hope that Ariadne's thread will bring you back one day.
I will wait on the cliff until I see the sails
of your returning ship.

BEAR

The advice they give you is …
if you meet a bear on the trail
stand as tall as you can
wave your arms and shout loud.

My cat, sleeping on the wall like a warm loaf,
knew exactly what to do
when a lolopy Labrador puppy dog passing by
excitedly stood and put his paws next to him,
and barked.
O'Malley (a fierce ginger tom)
stood as tall as he could and growled a growl
so deep and loud it seemed to come from China.
The dog, realizing his mistake, backed off
and, perhaps embarrassed,
peed on the lamppost as if to show he didn't care.

The advice I give you is …
always stand tall when you come across a bear
or a lolopy Labrador.

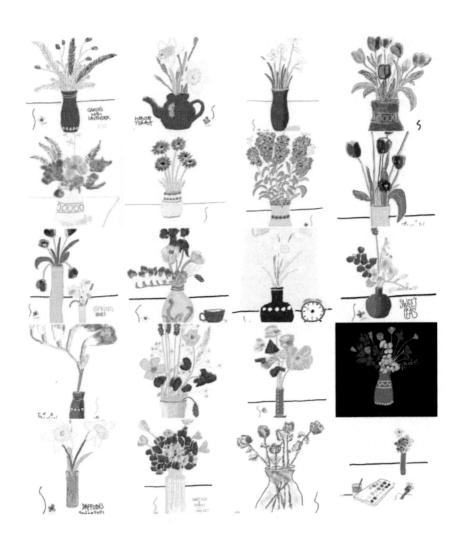

BABY

You certainly won't remember
but one of the very first things you saw
was the smile in your mother's happy eyes.
Ahead of you are years of love.
She will teach you
how to eat, to talk, to listen, to walk, and run,
and swim, and climb, and ride a bike.
She will read to you, hug you when you are hurt,
take you places.
She will sing songs to you and with you.
She will rub your back to help you sleep.
and will stay awake when you are sick.
She will cry on the first day you go to school.
Her heart will burst with pride when they read your name
and you walk across your graduation stages.

One day she will be sad when you leave.
I know.

MANY HAPPY RETURNS

When you open the shutters
on your birthday window
I hope you see YEARS of flowers ahead of you
in the different, separate gardens of your life:

the deep and passionate garden,

the bright, inspiring, and contented garden,

the quiet and thoughtful garden,
where the faces of old friends are reflected
in pools of memories,
the party garden littered with laughter
and loud music,
and your own special garden,
all of them filled with amazing vibrant colour.
Cats will purr all day,
dogs are sleeping, dreaming,
the sun has got his hat on and is coming out to play
-- NO shadows allowed anywhere.

And, oh, look up ...
even the clouds are dancing in your birthday sky.

MY NEW HAT

I insisted on Large.
The woman in the shop shook her head, "Medium
would be better, first gust of wind and
… POOF… It will be gone."
She mimed the event dramatically.
I insisted nevertheless on Large.
Inevitably, off it went
in the park one morning not long afterwards.

A young woman a hundred yards away caught it,
snatching it waist high
as casually and expertly
as a British Lions scrum half.
She smiled, one hand holding her hair
from tumbling across her face into her eyes,
and I wished she could have caught the thoughts
as easily that blew from my mind,
but the wind took them
… POOF ...
and I never saw her again.

sun
flowers
July '22

.303

I remember Sergeant Bryce.
His eyes were as blue as the sea
in the South of France but
could be as sharp as needles.
He showed us one afternoon
how to dismantle a rifle and clean it.
Sergeant Bryce held up his Lee Enfield .303
and asked:
What is this?
A soldier's personal weapon, sergeant, the reply
from all of us. We knew that. Yes.
But what is it FOR?
Erm erm er er, sergeant.
We didn't know the answer he wanted.
It is to KILL THE ENEMY.
The silence that shot into that room was immense.
To kill people?
GULP. Our Queen wants us to kill people?
Nooooooo. Not me, sergeant.

EACH MORNING

I love that
you take a fresh clean day
from the calendar cupboard,
you fill it with laughter and song
and paint it
with the bright colours of your busy life.

I also enjoy

that I have a box of yesterdays

to sit and dream about

with a cup of tea.

The Sycamore tree

A TREE IN ESSEX

From up here on the sixth floor
the sycamore tree down there
in the garden on the esplanade
looked as though she was dancing.
Some of the time a gentle swaying,
a Hawaiian hula,
but mostly frantically shaking,
waving her arms as if at a rock and roll concert,
completely involved in the rhythms
of a wind we couldn't feel behind our windows,
up here on the sixth floor.
All through the cold and wet winter,
she stood there naked, shivering,
the strength and the curves of her limbs,
and the elegance of her fragile fingers, unnoticed
by the cyclists struggling up the steep hill from the river.
by the joggers, by the parents with wrapped up children
passing on their way to somewhere else;
standing there, in the garden on the esplanade,
waiting for the daffodils to come and go,
waiting to wear her summer coat, to hear her leaves rustle,
to feel the rain, to dance in the wind, to be admired,
to give shade from the sun
and shelter from unexpected showers,
waiting for the parents with children to come and play
and sing and talk and have picnics on the grass,
and waiting for the cyclists
to rest at the top of the hill on the dark green park benches
drinking from their brightly coloured bottles.

THE WALK UP THE HILL

At the Equator on the day of the Equinox
there are no shadows
from the midday sun.
Here, though, this afternoon
the springtime sun was quite low behind us
as we walked up the hill,
our shadows stretching our legs
as they walked along with us,
as they ran ahead of us like excited spaniels.
There was no conversation between them;
they had no colour, no strong shapes.
They didn't show my beard,
or my favourite white scarf, your red lipstick,
the sparkling smile in your eyes from the wind,
the necklace that had been your grandmother's,
or that our boots were wet from walking in the grass.

On the way back down,
I saw that they followed us silently, as if sulking,
disappearing when the sun went behind a cloud.

POSTCARD
Scarborough. January.

The Ladies and the Gentlemen on the promenade
closed for the winter, locked.
The dodgem bumper cars silent,
still,
hibernating, waiting in dark tarpaulin caves
for the first bingo call of spring.
Milking machines rusting in quiet front parlours.
The sea tame as paper, the beach empty,
sand stretching
in long, cold, unbroken ribs.
Just one woman in a yellow coat
and a red knitted hat
throwing a ball for her dog, a black Labrador.
We sheltered from a shower in a doorway.
It made you smile
when I wrote in pencil on the wall
IT IS RAINING REALLY HARD
AND I LOVE YOU
VERY MUCH.

A TALE OF A COMET

THE TALE OF A COMET

visible above the horizon
in the evening sky of my life.

From the tail behind you,
sparkling particles of light have inspired me,
falling on the terrace of the cabin
next to the Sea of Imagination.
They shine into the room where I sit and write,
sprinkling ideas shaped like poems.
Often, I sit quietly with a glass of wine
listening to waves arriving like thoughts on the beach.
Each one excites the small pebbles who giggle
and race to follow
before being thrown back, still laughing,
by the next wave.
Occasionally, a piece of wood is left behind,
smallish and smooth as a perfect haiku.
Groups of pelicans glide effortlessly along the crests,
Sandpipers run in and out of the shallow surf,
reminding me of grandfathers
afraid their rolled-up trousers will get wet.

I think.
I am the beach; you are each wave.
We say to each other: don't worry,
I am here and I will be here tomorrow.
The small pebbles will giggle and race.
The sandpipers will run. The pelicans will glide.

THE 17.45

They had agreed to meet at four
in that small café
just off The Strand, near Trafalgar Square.
It was a grey, quite cold day, damp and drizzling,
dreech as the Scots so perfectly describe it.
She was late as she almost always was, he remembered,
but, when her smile came in, the room was suddenly alive,
even the dark blue of the carpet seemed more intense.

She ordered one of those green herbal teas,
Orange Jasmine, Purple Blueberry, or Mango Pineapple,
something exotic or bizarre that vegan girls tend to drink.
He chose Darjeeling, his favourite in the afternoon.

She ate a slice of Victoria Sponge Cake
delicately with a small fork.
There was a moment when a smudge of jam
stayed on her cheek next to her mouth,
and she wiped it off
without pausing from her telling of the story
of spending Christmas with her Great Aunt Maud
in Shropshire.
He picked up his Eccles Cake with his fingers
and ate it like a savage, enjoying every bite,
the puff pastry, the sugar, the fruit and spices
sticky on his fingers and his lips.

They laughed and sometimes sighed silently,

they talked and talked of the time, many years before,
when they had been lovers.
"I must go," she said after a while,
"If I miss the train at 17.45, I will have to wait an hour."

As he walked alone along The Strand,
his umbrella in his hand, enjoying the reflections
of the lights from buses dancing in the rain,
a memory came back to him
of watching a film with his daughter who was four,
an old Betjeman documentary in black and white
about steam trains and small country stations
in Somerset.
At the end she had asked, seriously,
"What was it like, Daddy, before there was colour?"

"Well," he had replied,
"it's love that makes the colour in our lives.
But as time passes it can fade away."

MARCH in JUNE 2020. Black Cats Matter Too

Considered old and delicate at 80,
I am sheltering in my hillside home,
safely distanced from the Covid particles and droplets
flying from the mouths of a thousand demonstrators.
I can hear police sirens, see the helicopters circling.
My arms don't ache from holding a sign.
My throat isn't sore from shouting.
My legs don't hurt, but my tears and the pain I feel
are just as real.
I am content now to allow young people
who are alive and awake to change the world
I have sadly merely mumbled and grumbled about.

Down there,
masked gangs ambush a chanting procession
to offer hand sanitizer and bottled water,
and watch as a singing, shouting, marching mural
slides by, an animated tapestry
hoping to inspire the leaders who parked
the National Guard at the high school on Melrose Avenue,
hoping to inspire those leaders to sit, and think, and talk,
and fix this cracked and broken America.

Up here
the red and pink sweet peas pose,
delicate in a pale blue vase,
and the lizard outside on the window ledge
is teasing our black cat.

LONDON

She had moved recently to Maida Vale.
I called to see if I could visit.

Yes, please come, she told me on the telephone.
She was at home alone, she said,
entertaining her cat.

Was she wearing a long frock, I wondered,
with jewels, tiara, and silver high-heeled shoes,
serving chilled creamy milk, straight from the fridge,
with pink salmon, pilchards, and garlic
-- being careful not to stain her white lace gloves?

Or did she mean dressed up

with a red nose, starred eyes, and fishnet tights,

unicycling around her room,
balancing a glass of red wine
on a silver tray in one hand
while reading aloud from The Lord of the Rings?

Maybe just singing gently something
from Dire Straits?

A CANDLE
with
SWEET
PEAS
&
POPPIES
I

PRONOUNCED 'DEAD'
(For a friend who lost a loved one during Lockdown)

You watched as sadness was being crystalised,
the biting wind blowing flakes of pain and loneliness
into deep drifts.
The footprints that she left in the snow
will never disappear like those we leave each day
in the daily blizzard of our daily lives.

She will be there
when you feel the sun warm on your wrist,
driving in your car, sitting on a bus,
in the shape of the window shining
on the wall of your room or on the floor.
She will be there
when you hear a door close in another room,
when the phone rings on a Sunday morning.
She will be there
sitting on the sideways smile of the moon
waving
as it quietly slides across the daytime sky.
She will be there every day
on the mourning train of thoughts
that stops at your station.

She is gone but she isn't.

LIBERTY

Un Mélange

. poèmes

.. pensées

... peintures

My first words of French were:
"Cette sauce de haute qualité
est un mélange de fruits orientaux…"

I was 9. I read the label, at the table
of the HP sauce bottle,
in English on one side, French on the other.

I remembered those words as I began assembling this
cheerful, charming collection of my recent pomes & pikchas.
Un mélange, yes, I thought that is exactly what this is.

SAD SUNFLOWERS

BIRD

There are times when the bird
in my bedroom sings silently in the night.
I like that I can go to my vocabulary,
collect some bags of words
and share his songs.

One picture, they say,
is worth a thousand words
but my yellow bird doesn't sing pictures.
He sings ideas, thoughts and memories.
I wrap them in words,
never a thousand, though,
and give them as a gift to you.

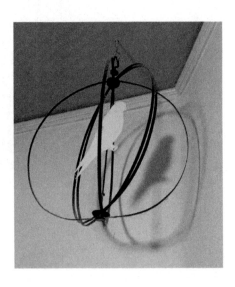

YORKSHIRE
Sept 21

DOWN
END
Hook Norton
Oct 2021

ST IVES

1.22 WAIMEA #1
PARKER RANCH

WINDOW
in WORDSDALE

JANUARY

It rained in LA last night.
A tickle at the foot of the dark mountain
of my midnight room woke me.
A trickle of sounds ….
ticking like a loud grandfather clock,
tapping on the roof of the house next door,
typing on the leaves of a bush,
splashing down the steps outside my window,
drumming of gusts of raindrops
thrown against the glass by the wind.
A wide river of sounds
burst the banks of my quiet sleep.
I could see (with my eyes closed)
whole poems rushing past in the flood ….
long boats of narrative sagas,
sweet, happy, little rhyming couplets, holding hands,
iambic pentameters chanting,
even a haiku paddling past counting syllables,
and off to the side, a cascade, singing a song
as it dropped down a worderfall
into a deep pool of love,
where kisses swam like fishes,
some large and slow, others just tiny gold flashes.

And then … the sound of a jet taking off from LAX
drowned the water. The flood was over.
The room was dark again and quiet.
Just the light from my silent clock that said 00.43.

RED ROSE
sweet pea
&
cup of tea

THE GARDEN OF MY AUNT

Le jardin de ma tante

When they demolished the Catholic Church
on the corner by the new shops a few years ago,
my auntie bought a small statue for two pounds 50.
She thought it was a bargain.
It was slightly chipped, but she repainted
the hair and beard with some brown gloss
she had in her spare room.
One hand was holding its lapel like a teacher.
My auntie planted her plaster Jesus
In her garden in the middle of her pansies.
She said the yellow of the flowers went well
with the purple of his robe.
He is still there at the edge of the pond, preaching
to a small congregation of plastic gnomes with red hats.

They have built another church now
on the spare land near the entrance to the estate.
Jesus cost over 500 pounds, they say.
He is stainless steel.

AN UNANSWERED QUESTION

But, no, tell me WHY you write, the woman asked,
smiling.
Do you write to describe an experience we have shared,
to paint a picture,
to bring me the colours of a place I haven't seen,
the quality of a feeling,
the excitement of an event,
the tension of a meeting?
Do you write to play with language,
to alliterate, to rhyme, to gallop, chasing words along a line?
Do you write to philosophise, to give an opinion,
to agree or disagree?
Do you write for me or for some unseen muse
a thousand miles away?
Or do you write merely to enjoy
the poetry and the rhythm of your words?

THE LABELING OF LOOS

I noticed on the Isle of Skye

that the MacLeods, in the north,

are quite polite, have Toilets.
in their Dunvegan Castle.
for LADIES and GENTLEMEN.
In the south, though,
at Armadale, the castle of the MacDonalds,

there are Lavatories. LADIES, yes, true,

where the girls take sweet pees
and have flowers and hand lotion

and mirrors for them to modify and beautify themselves,

but at the end of a long corridor is the sign
MEN.
In there, REAL men,
MacDonald men, don't do zips and stuff …
they simply lift their kilts, and afterwards wash their hands
under a tap of freezing water.
Real MEN, aye, over there in Skye,
that's what they do
at the loo.

46

DAFFODIL
spring
'22

sun
flowers
2021

BIRDS OF
PARADISE
LAVENDER
&
JONQUILS
Feb 22

APRIL
MMXXII

47

ISLAND QUEEN

"I sometimes wonder if she was really a mermaid."

We were sitting at the bar at the Island Queen in Islington. I was halfway down a pint of Guinness, and she was sipping a glass of Chardonnay. We were talking about her grandmother who, she said, liked to swim in the sea each morning all year around with a group of friends.

"But, I mean, just because she liked to swim in the sea in January doesn't mean she was a mermaid, does it? Do you think her friends were mermaids, too?"

She took a couple of Salt and Vinegar crisps from the torn open packet on the bar and crunched them for a minute. "No, I suppose not, but it was just something about her, and now it's too late. She died last March so I can't ask."

"Well, I suppose she didn't have a tail. Did she have a seashell mirror and sit brushing her long golden hair? Did she avoid eating fish and chips?"

"No, nothing like that. She just, I don't know how to say it, she just could tell things, she could predict, she knew stuff that was going to happen."
She reached up with both hands, gathered her hair together and put it into a ponytail, twisting the elastic a couple of times. It's a girl thing I always find very attractive, the speed it takes and how easy it looks.
"And anyway, it is well known that a mermaid can take human form. The Selkies in Scotland do it, and it it happens in Norway and Russia too with the huldra and rusalka."

Although her eyes were smiling there was a slight edge to her tone, like I shouldn't make fun.

"Sorry, I was teasing. She was your father's mother, right? Have you ever talked about it to him?"

"Not really, not *that* idea. I knew about his life and stuff, but he didn't speak about his parents, and we only saw them at Christmas and the summer holidays. I remember my grandfather; he smoked a pipe. I would love to sit on his knee when I was little to watch him cleaning it and cutting tobacco from long strings with a sharp penknife, rubbing it in his old cracked hands, stuffing the pipe and lighting it from a big box of matches, Swan Vestas they were called, and sitting back in his chair puffing, relighting, and sometimes gently blowing smoke in my face to make me laugh and cough. He would play an accordion and sing old sea shanties, and he taught my sister and me how to dance jigs and reels. He had been a sailor all his life and the story we knew was that he had met my grandmother during the war when he was in the Navy, stationed in Cornwall, and had later married her and they moved together to Suffolk where he had grown up. He died while I was at university."

She stopped for a minute and crunched a few more crisps. It seemed she needed a minute to go back to remembering her grandfather.
We both drank from our glasses, she with small sips, me slurping my pint wiping my beard afterwards with the back of my hand. We ate more crisps, finishing the packet.

"So, tell me more about your idea that your grandmother was a mermaid."

"Well … things. There was never any mention of her parents, of her family. No photos. No stories. All we knew was that she was from a small village in West Cornwall."

"But ..."

"I know, it just fitted the idea. And then there was the way she knew stuff."

"Stuff? Like ... what?"

"Like there was a time when my parents were first married, they went to Suffolk for Christmas and as they were leaving she hugged my mother and whispered, "you will have twins." My mother didn't even know she was pregnant at the time. Then she added "and they will be girls and will be very special." And it's true!"
She stopped, and smiled, turning towards me and opening her arms.
"Don't you think I'm special?"

I really only knew her from work, we were both teachers at the high school round the corner, but, yes, I could see that she would be considered special.

"Well, er, yes, as a matter of fact yes."

I could feel my face getting hot. I have always been teased for blushing.

"So ..." Changing the subject often helped.

"But tell me, how did we get on to the subject of your grandmother? We were talking about that small group of girls in Year 11 who somehow manage to sabotage every lesson. I went and bought the crisps and you were miles away when I came back and opened them. And, dadah, in steps Granny."

"Well, I was sitting here looking at the shelves behind the bar and the glasses all lined up in their different sizes. And I remembered my grandmother telling me that she will always be close to me. Look at the stars in the sky, she had said, look for groups of daffodils in the park, look for sheep or cows in a field, look for flocks of geese, or starlings, watch waves at the beach, I will be there, each one is a kiss from me. When the traffic light changes to green, that's me, I am there. And as I looked at the glasses on the shelf, there she was."

FLOWER
PIE

SOMEDAY IS NOT A DAY OF THE WEEK

It was the moon that started it,
whizzing round the earth in 28 days exactly, precisely,
predictably waxing and waning.
Then that Eve bit that apple in that garden
and women began to cycle too.
But it was really the Sumerians about 5000 years ago
who divided time into weeks and days and hours
and minutes by whimsically
counting the knuckles on their fingers,
and giving a name to each separate day.
They didn't, though, leave room in any of their weeks
for a Someday.
For centuries expeditions looked for that lost day.
Greeks philosophized,
Phoenicians voyaged,
Babylonians studied the stars and isosceles triangles,
Trojans pillaged and built wooden horses,
Romans tried ides,
Russians and the French had revolutions,
Crowds of Christian knights crusaded to Jerusalem,
St Patrick killed all the snakes in Ireland.
Vikings raped and plundered, Leonardo da Vinci wondered,
Columbus searched in America,
Sir Francis Drake sailed around the world,
Dr. Livingstone followed the River Nile,
At Livermore an atom was split,
Neil Armstrong took a giant step.

In early 1989 delegates at a convention in Hawaii,

enjoyed the beach and drank mai tais at sunset.
They argued and disagreed, as experts often do,
and in the end decided that talking about Someday
was really like expecting world peace
or equal treatment and respect for all human beings.

HUALALAI
A retired, sleeping
volcano
— from my lanai —

MAUNA
KEA BEACH

BEADS

I have photos on my phone,
but I have pictures in my mind.
Goats on a golf course,
breeze in the trees, horses on a hill,
waves rushing, swishing, whales' tails splashing,
flowers in a field,
a turtle sleeping on a bed of black lava,
the sun ….
white in the morning climbing up over the mountain,
red in the evening snuggling down into its horizon.
Each picture a bead in a necklace of memories
of a holiday in Hawaii.

BY THE LIGHT OF THE SLIVERY MOON

It was there again early this morning, the moon. Well really just a very thin, slight tear in the curtain of the dark, grey sky, just above the horizon.

I wanted to tiptoe up, look through and see what was inside.

Maybe, I imagined … Stars and starlets in long frocks and jewels still celebrating a jolly good Hollywood event.

The chefs at the Café Chez Les Etoiles working on their plât du jour, chopping, slicing, mixing, tasting, even singing from time to time, their pans bubbling, steaming, sizzling.

Television traffic anchors, lipstick and tight dresses, preparing their illuminated mosaics, pressing red lights on to maps of motorways, freeways, autobahns, autoroutes, autostradas, and sensually stroking the curves of their diagrams of gusts of wind, barometric pressure, and topical depressions.

Dreams being boxed ready to be despatched, some straightaway as day dreams, to buses, trains, farms, offices, factories, and schools, others being sent off to dance later in the dark of a thousand bedrooms, others on horseback, night mares, to gallop into anxious minds.

A peloton of cyclists on the Tour des Etoiles swooping like a flock of starlings along the Milky Way, riders shouting, spectators cheering, drowning the sound of the swishing of the tires on the crystal roadway.

In the distance a river which had already flowed into the
afternoon, children splashing, families with picnic
sandwiches, folding chairs, and dogs that barked.

But it is twenty-five to six and the sun
is lighting the sky ready to begin the day.

A LUNA TRICK

I met a woman once on a train
who told me she writes on the moon
when it is wide and full.
The words of a song sometimes,
a gem of wisdom,
a philosophical nugget,
a message of love.

Why not? she said,
the words go all around the world

and it's free.

JUST A THOUGHT

If he had stayed indoors that autumn afternoon instead of sitting reading under that apple tree, would we have ever known about the concept of gravity, I wonder? What if that apple had not dropped at that moment at that spot and he had finished the chapter and gone indoors for a cup of tea and a scone with jam?

Isaac Newton had been sent to work from home when Cambridge University closed in 1665 for several years because of the plague. It is unlikely that he would have ever connected the story of King Knute and the unstoppable tide with the apple, the moon and gravity. I don't suppose many children went to the seaside in the 1600s. Nowadays, of course, every child who has spent time at the beach building sandcastles and digging holes knows that the tide will come in, but certainly would not think of the moon when their castles are flooded, their ramparts overwhelmed and torn down by an incoming whooshing wave.

But it's true. The gravity of the moon changes the level of the oceans every day and has done so for millions of years. That dear old moon races around the earth, beginning as a thin smile hardly noticed in the daytime sky, growing each night, each day, until the night of the mighty full moon. It is as spectacular as a rocket launch, as a baby being born. The huge full moon fills a familiar horizon, a city, mountain, forest, plain. You can actually see it moving as it rises. Full moons are celebrities, and have names, the same every year, given to them centuries ago — a Pink Moon, a Wolf Moon, a Flower Moon, a Harvest Moon. There are Strawberry and Cold Moons, and quite occasionally and rarely there is a Blue Moon.

Being dry, and, I guess, thirsty, the moon tries to suck water from our oceans and that's what makes the tide. Gravity, that's what it is. It's hard though to connect the dots between an apple in an orchard in Lincolnshire 400 years ago, a sandcastle in Santa Monica today, and the man in the moon.

POEM*EOP*

The idea came in the night for the poem to write for a friend. It would be clever, a play on one of those words that has two meanings, like gravity, or motion, or set, but then the word went away this afternoon. Evaporated. It had gone, just when I needed it to help me write.

On my walk I meet Ann and her dog a couple of times a week maybe. She lives round the corner halfway up the hill,has white hair, writes children's books, and sometimes wears a bright green coat. We stop usually and have one of those 'neighbours passing in the street' conversations. The dog is extraordinarily happy, always finding something to investigate, always with a greeting lick and an excited tail as I stroke her bony head and scratch her ears while we chat, Ann and I. Every time I have forgotten her name, but she doesn't mind. MOLLIE, MOLLIE, yes, of course. MOLLIE. There are other dogs on my walk that are like mechanical toys. Those guys, and their android walkers, don't look at me, don't acknowledge me, don't even see me, I think. They are in the fast lane, counting their steps. They know where they are going and that's where they are going.They'll be there before they know where they are.

So, it's a little disturbing, this forgetting thing with words, because it hasn't just been unusual words like coagulate, exasperate, exacerbate, procrastinate, or the name of the capital of Pakistan, or Kentucky that I can't find. On the big highways I'm fine, usually, I can drive along the sentences at around 80 wpm. My fingers know the way to ASDF JKL; I do get lost though these days, as I am older, looking for the creative villages where poems live. And that's exactly what's happened here. I'm on the way to the birthday poem and I can't find the address, the word that has my idea in it.

I make a cup of tea and go to sit in my …. er, you know, the place I sit in, next to the … er, you know, the place where you can see outside. What is that damn word? It's an image, a copy, er, but well not a copy exactly. In England we use "inverted commas" to show quotes. A speech begins with a 66 ... listen, pay attention and ends with its opposite, a 99, a firm, strong end. Opposite, yes, but that's not the word. Looking in a mirror, your left eye is really your right eye, and your right hand is really your left hand. What's that called? If you stand near a lake or a river there is a you, in the water, wobbly and long but it's a you. What is that called? It's on the tip of my tongue. It's a .....
No. Don't tell me.

I sit and drink my tea and sit and think, and ponder, and er, you know, and it's there, OMG the word!!! I have been sitting in my, er, chair REFLECTING, and right in front of me I see my, you know, my REFLECTION in the er, the window.
Now I must, er, write the er, you know, the thing.
The poem,'REFLECTIONS'.

The er … chair

SUMMER
2021

FRANK WILKINSON
(Britain's entry for next year's human race)

A boat stood on a hill near Ross on Wye.
It had no name. There was a house, some trees,
a small, red, child's tricycle, no elephants
or kangaroos. Potatoes grew in rows.
The house was numbered 53 but there were no others.
A woman wearing blue rubber gloves
was painting a fence as I drove past.
I'm almost sure she smiled.

Down at the foot of the hillside
      STEEP ---- KEEP
      IN LOW GEAR
in the town I had to stop at a traffic light.
I saw a man with a beard and a guitar singing to himself
in a room above a butcher's shop.

Before the light changed to green
and I continued on to Birmingham
there was a moment, a strange moment.
He looked at me, put down his guitar, came to the window,
and his eyes sang this song, told me this story ....

"I live near here and I've built a boat because
next year at the equinox, at Michaelmas,
there is going to be a flood and you'll all die.
But I'll be alright
        GOD chose me and I know why.
Because ... I am a vegetarian
Because ...I hardly ever watch television
Because ... I dig my own garden
Because … I don't believe in organised religion.
I think it should be personal, like hygiene.
You do or you don't, it's up to you.

I had this vision, you see, after one day, years ago,
a green Ford Transit van stopped outside my house,
number 53, up there at the top of the hill.

The driver ... a West Indian, tall he was,
had sunglasses and a black shirt with silver threads
that sparkled in the sun when he moved,
gave me his card; it said simply

God
in gold gothic letters with a capital G.

He spoke:
"Look, man,
I'm just sick of hearin' 'bout war and hunger and
plane crashes
and refugees and urban decay and killin' and

depletion of the ozone layer.
"LOOK" he said, "I am GOD and I tell you – I am goin
to stop all this
and start again wid YOU, man. So,
listen carefully … Find yourself a girl called Marilyn
marry her and have a kid." So,
I did. She had a boy.
We called him Jesus Noah Wilkinson. He's ten.

"Now," God cleared his throat, and
wiped his nose with a tissue
from a box he had on the dash in his van.
"I want you to build a boat here in your front garden,
collect a few animals, a couple of butterflies,
some seeds, and useful things like a candle, a pencil,
a needle, a novel, maybe a jewel or two,
because when your kid is old enough, like eleven,
I'll nip down from Heaven and start the rain.
Heavy it will be. Quite soon
your lovely view of Gloucestershire and
Herefordshire will disappear
under water, but you just sit in the boat.
Don't worry, Frank, it will float. I'll see you right.
            They will all die
            But you'll be OK."
Then he drove away.
He had some angels in his green Transit van.
I saw their long hair and heard them sing …
"Frank Wilkinson,
he digs his own garden,
and he is a vegetarian."

A ROOFING MAN

From where I was sitting
I could see through the window
a man on the roof of the cottage next door.
He walked confidently and casually,
could almost have been with his dog in the park
in the evening after work.
I even imagined him singing to himself.
He carried a bucket,
an essential, I'm sure, for repairing roofs.
Myself, I would have been bent over, i think,
perhaps crawling, afraid of falling to the ground
or crashing through into a bedroom,
or, more embarrassing,
to surprise someone in the bath.
He knew though, that, of all the workers on the site,
he was THE ROOFER, the king,
and he walked accordingly.

BLUE
VASE

7 MAY 1992

It was almost an hour from Orlando to Cape Canaveral. It was dark when we arrived and parked on the side of the road. 6:25. We had made it. The launch of the new shuttle Endeavour was due at 6:30.

We got out of the car. It was as though all the air had been sucked away by the excitement of the crowd. Then, it began. At first the ground vibrated, then the sound came across the fields as though the world was splitting open. A small fire was visible which grew as the rocket climbed away from its nest. For what seemed an hour it just stood there balancing on that bright light, before, feeling comfortable, it rose so slowly, shaking the clouds off like drops in the shower. The sound was unique, a crackle that just shook the whole earth. The rocket went up and up curving overhead until my neck hurt following it.

The world came back then, settling like a lake after the ripple flattened from the stone you had thrown. We stood there, not wanting to talk, not even able to find words.

The astronauts were still riding that vibrating racing dragon, flying into space as we drove back on the 528, stopping to feed the horses and have coffee and a chicken sandwich. Those guys calmly checked their systems and flew by at 17,000 mph.

PRIMROSE

You stand so tall,
like a little girl on her way to school,
face looking up, clean and happy,
reflecting the sunshine,
the anticipation
of the enjoyment of the day ahead.

Primrose,
you are quite small
but I can feel your strength.
It is inspiring.

THE SHIP

The whole town has come out to watch
this day, this Wednesday morning
From a grey ocean where waves
were as tall as trees, and days were as long as weeks,
a small ship arrives in the port
The captain is anxious to unload its cargo,
packets of refrigerated memories,
of remarkable, memorable moments
squeezed and sliced into sentences.
As she takes the packets and snips them open
words pour on to the quayside, well, the table in Room B2.
Some, brightly dressed, dance enthusiastically,
others offer warm tableaux of love, of babies, of mothers,
of magnolia trees, of cats, of festivals,
of childhood and old houses.

There are bands of today's and yesterday's stories,

marching in columns.
And then a tsunami storm of a sad experience
bursts from its packet, raging and racing,
stripping the smiles from spectators,
shredding, scattering their tears, leaving behind it
a silence.

(Barnsdall Arts Center, LA.
A pre-Covid creative writing class,
The reading of work.)

NAKED EYE

When I heard an expert on the radio say
"They are invisible to the naked eye."
I wondered what she meant.
Can they only be seen by motorcyclists
wearing goggles, or by huddles of
astronomers in observatories on remote
mountain tops in South America,
who can Hubble them, whatever they are.

And.
What exactly IS a naked eye?
Are thoughts, for example,
invisible to the naked eye
until they are translated into poetry
and printed on a page?

TWO DAYS IN NOVEMBER ... TUESDAY 23rd

People have told me I have "kind" eyes. Silly, how can EYES be kind? The doctor, though, said that they are close to their UseByDate and tomorrow, Wednesday, is going to take out the lenses I have used all my life and "just" pop in silicone ones made in South Texas.

My eyes have been to so many places, from Aberdeen to West Wittering and Washington DC. They watched my daughters being born. They exchanged smiles once with Jimmy Carter and Kate Beckinsale, and many times with strangers. They saw snow in Yosemite, have been the long way to Tipperary, have felt strong November Cornish gales, warm Hawaiian Trade Winds, and hot, dry California Santa Anas. They read books, watched films and plays. They have seen thunderstorms, the Northern Lights in Inverness, and Hayley's Comet. They saw lovers naked with no clothes on, Sequoia trees, the Matterhorn, Ben Nevis, the Rocky Mountains, Old Faithful, and the Mojave Desert, 1000 sunsets, full moons rising, MilkyWays of stars, and flowers in gardens and wild, waving as I drove by. Once they saw the Queen in a car at a traffic light in Plymouth, but she was talking and didn't see me. They have sparkled when happy and laughed a lot. They have cried at funerals, weddings, graduations, and concerts. Occasionally but rarely, they have been angry, sometimes quite sad, but mostly aware and alive.

So, around noon (Pacific Time) Wednesday think of me, hold my hand, please, (I am a total baby) as my new eyes are being 'popped in'. I hope they will know how to smile and will be as kind as the old ones that will be thrown away.

TWO DAYS IN NOVEMBER … THURSDAY 25th
(Thanksgiving Day)

Blast!! That's what I picked from my box of words to describe this day. My father, in his wonderful old-fashioned way, surprising for an old professional soldier, would have said that 'Blast' is a swearword. I think though that what I mean is more like an explosion.

Flying gently in the breeze from the open window, the fuzzy dragons who normally patrol the skies above my bed, this morning were alive, sharp, bright red, blue, and green. The stitched-on smile on the bear's face, always positive, but perhaps a little vague, this morning was strong and definite.

The books standing quietly on their shelves, usually just shapes, this morning were individuals, all with titles which I could read. This morning, the blurred blobs of the collection of my floral watercolours were sharp, a summer garden in my bedroom.

I could see the small blue squeeze of toothpaste on the brush when I cleaned my teeth. In the mirror my eyes smiled.

I went to the kitchen to make my morning cup of tea. The intensity, the brightness, the preciseness of the leaves of the plants, the ornaments in the window, even the spice jars, the flowers, and spider webs I hadn't seen before, everything! It overwhelmed. I couldn't speak, I wanted to cry.

The view from my Breakfast Window on this Santa Ana morning was breathtaking. The detail. The colours, the houses on the hill below, the five palm trees, and the streets so clear. Western Avenue all the way to the horizon, a good 30 miles or so. The buildings of downtown like teeth biting the sky. I could see a constant line of aircraft on their way to land at LAX. I could see the Vincent Thomas Bridge and the outlines of the cranes at the port of San Pedro. I could see Santa Catalina Island 50 miles away so clearly…

When the doctor had sliced my eyes, taken out the worn-out parts and dropped in these new amazing lenses, made in Texas, I was afraid I would lose the smiles I had learned to use in our world of masks, but he replaced them with loud shouts of laughter.

My new world is so bright my lenses even have a UV coating to protect me from strong sunlight.

Castle Feliz, Los Angeles, Nash dom.

Two Little Ducks

(The Bingo Call for Number 22)

Here are 22 poems from 2022 … MMXXII

Kelly's Eye, number 1,
Doctor's Orders, number 9,
Clickety Click, 66,
Key of the Door, 21,
Two Little Ducks, 22.

B I N G O !!

Tiptoe …..

SWEET PEAS
AFRICAN
DAISIES
CALIFORNIA
POPPIES

APRIL
FLOWERS

GRASSES
WITH
LAVENDER

2-21

85

ALWAYS

I can think of lots of ways

to avoid writing.
I frequently sit comfortably
with a cup of tea,
sipping.

Here I am today

listening to the clock.

As it ticks
I count backwards
from 100 in fives.

A TREE IN WORDSDALE

Only a few leaves left blowing
on the tree next to the gate.
A handful, 4, maybe 5, or 6.
Brown, yellow,
they will go soon, I am sure,
perhaps this afternoon
if it rains.

"There's always one, isn't there? people say.

This small group of leaves,
who have spent the spring and summer together,
are not quite ready yet
to fall and be mulched.

AGINCOURT

I almost died when I was nine,
my mother told me.
Pneumonia.
All I can remember is reading a book, sitting in my bed,
a book with thick grey covers and pages with ragged edges,
about the battle of Agincourt,
how the English archers beat the French.
An arrow fired from a longbow, I learned then
and have never forgotten,
could penetrate the armour of a mounted knight,
go right through his leg
and into his horse.

So,
that's my memory of pneumonia.
Oh,
and the giant penicillin tablets,
which, even cut in half,
were very difficult to swallow.

"Yes,
you almost died in that cold, cold winter of 1949,"
my mother told me, adding, with a smile,
"but almost isn't quite."

I WAS TEN

I took the bus to school from the edge of the city
into town.
I liked to sit downstairs at the front
behind the driver.

In Kings Heath,
just after the railway station,
there was a roundabout, a sharp turn.
The driver loved it,
racing the motor to change down
to take the bend as fast as possible.
We could see him in his cab
leaning way over to the right in his seat
to balance the weight of the double decker bus
almost toppling over,
imagining himself, perhaps,
a member of the crew
of a racing yacht, rounding the final buoy,
smiling with satisfaction
as we swept up the steep little hill in second gear

towards the Rugby Ground at the top,

past the row of houses that had been bombed,

one with part of the staircase

hanging next to what had been a bedroom

with purple flowered wallpaper.

The conductor, on his platform at the back of the bus,
would shout at the top of his voice, every morning the same,

"Hold tight around the bend!
Hang on to your parrots and monkeys!" **

I didn't understand. I asked my mother.
"Oh well," she said, "you see, before the war ...."

I heard that all the time,
"Before the war .... Before the war ... Before the war"
as if it had been perfect,
and I never did believe it.
Life could not be better than it was for me,
10 years old.

** *'Pick up your parrots and monkeys and fall in*
facing the boat' was the traditional last order given
to a detachment of British soldiers heading home
from India.

SLOW DOWN

slow down, you are eating like a wolf,
my mother said once, at dinner time, I remember.
Eat gently, chew your meat a hundred times
before you swallow.
(Well, alright, maybe she really said twenty).

How did she know back then, in 1951?

There was no internet, no television.
How did we know anything at all?
Sir David Attenborough was still at university,
learning.
The Pictorial Knowledge Encyclopedia,
on the bookshelf in the front room did have
at the end of each volume wonderful pop-up diagrams
which opened up to show:
the parts of the human digestive system,
the inside of a steam railway locomotive,
an internal combustion engine, a volcano,
all brightly coloured, labelled, and numbered, with a key.
No mention anywhere, though, I am pretty sure,
of wolves savagely attacking mashed potatoes and peas,
or blackberry and apple crumble with custard.

There were no wolves
in the woods of suburban Birmingham.
We didn't hear them howling at the moon at night.
Sometimes, perhaps, the corgi next door
barking at the wind,
or Mrs Appleby's chickens in her back garden
at number 77
grumbling quietly before they went to sleep.
Certainly, no wolves.

How then
did she know the eating habits of North American wolves,
for goodness' sake?
I mean, my mother was from Manchester, England.

AFTER THE DROUGHT

the recent heavy winter rains
have washed away the words;
even my muse has long gone
not leaving one single syllable
for me to nibble

sometimes in the night
an idea is there in the dark:
the similarities & differences
of alone & lonely
for example

but the following day
the idea struggles scratches and bites
refusing to be dressed in words;
the me I am leaves it be
& has a cup of tea or maybe takes a short walk
to the end of the street …
my daughter Rose –being familiar with gadgets
as young people tend to be – has measured that walk:
quarter of a mile there and back
so 4 times would be a mile
she tells me

I am content with just once walking briskly
believing that to be quite sufficient
for a man of my age with arthritis in my left shoulder
& I find something else…
some perfectly good reason to sit
and **not** address
being alone does not equal being lonely
imagining how it might be discussed
in not less than six lines
sitting at some schoolroom desk

the words will be there tomorrow I am sure
sitting quietly in their stanzas
waiting to be read aloud

perhaps I'll take the iPad and its pencil
just like I did yesterday
and paint a daffodil

I REMEMBER THE FIFTH OF NOVEMBER

Not long ago, I was looking in my wardrobe, planning to thin out the shirts and coats, and give the ones I never wore to a charity shop. I found a green M&S (Marks and Spencer) waxed coat ... I had bought it over 30 years ago in England, in Brighton. I tried it on. In the pocket were some strands of lavender. I had picked them in a park in Rottingdean and had sat on a bench and cried the day before my mother died. I feel the tightness in my throat now as I sit typing. My mother was dying from pancreatic and liver cancer.

My father hadn't told me that she was ill until the day before she was to be discharged from the hospital. I had immediately flown from my home in Los Angeles to Gatwick. As my taxi pulled up at the house, there was an ambulance there. The driver had just opened the rear door and was pulling out the stretcher. When my mother saw me standing there, her face just lit up. A special moment.

The first two days, she mostly slept, like a cat. Quietly. I made a lamb stew, one of her favourites, with bones from the butcher in the village, carrots, potatoes, a little celery, a few other bits and bobs, as she would have said, a generous sprinkle or two of pepper, and a few sultanas just as she always did. I managed to feed her a few spoonfuls, but she almost immediately threw them up. She was incredibly thin and couldn't wear her teeth. My mother. The woman who would go nowhere without lipstick, a silk scarf, and usually a hat. Mostly she slept. There were intervals when she was awake, talking to the mirror of the dressing table across the room as if it was her mother and her sister there, visiting, standing at the foot of her bed. But mostly, she slept like a cat.

As I opened the curtains, the November Fifth morning sun was a deep red as it climbed slowly above the Saltdean Hotel on the hill opposite, throwing off the mist-like covers from its bed in the park in the valley. I went back to my mother's bedside and moved her pillows so that she could sit up. "I made you a cup of tea." Her smile was weak, really a soft thank you from her eyes. We sat quietly for a long minute, watching the sun rise together. She couldn't hold a cup with a saucer, so I held the cup to her lips and tilted small sips into her toothless mouth. She had never spent a day without her teeth or her glasses. I stayed with her as she dozed quietly, like a cat. Mid-morning, she asked me to help her with the bedpan. It had always been a quiet joke with my father when we sat in the evening after our cup of Ovaltine or Bournville Cocoa, made with milk and a couple of digestive or rich tea biscuits, when she would go to clean her teeth and brush her hair ready for bed, that we would hear her lock the bathroom door. He had told me once, "She even does it when it's just the two of us here!" And now here I was, lifting my naked mother, a bag of bones thinner than pencils, onto a bedpan and wiping her very private 'down there', a part that didn't have a name in her house in my life.

Nurses had been coming to visit to take care of her. It was obvious that the pain was getting worse. The doctor had called and had arranged for a nurse to come and stay full-time at the house. Nurse Murphy came in the afternoon and immediately sent me to the chemist with a prescription for morphine.

Around six o'clock, after the sun had set, the curtains were closed again, and there were sounds of fireworks exploding around the neighbourhood. I sat at the small kitchen table and silently nibbled at the lamb stew with my father, who was in a trance, exhausted and unbelieving. Neither of us were hungry, really. I took the dishes and spoons, washed and dried them and put them in the cupboard, just as she would have done.

97

Our cups of tea, untouched, went cold.

The nurse gave her a morphine injection and stayed in the bedroom with her. She suggested that we both try to lie down and take a rest. It was almost midnight when she woke us. "You should come into the bedroom, she's going." Her breathing was slow and difficult. She was awake but grey and still. I held her hand, cold and bony. "Cold hands, warm heart," I whispered.

She looked at me, that same warm, soft smile from her eyes that came from a long way away. She coughed a delicate cough, and that was it. She was gone. Her face relaxed; the pain was over.

"Remember, remember, The Fifth of November," the children call at bus stops and outside supermarkets raising money for fireworks. They celebrate the night in 1605, the discovery of The Gunpowder Plot, with bonfires, rockets, and Catherine wheels, the night when Sir Thomas Knyvet and a handful of Justices of the Peace went to the cellar of the Palace of Westminster, and found Guy Fawkes, with a group of Roman Catholic noblemen who wanted to restore their Church as the established Church of England, sitting with lighted candles next to 36 barrels of gunpowder, over 2 tons of dynamite, waiting to blow up and kill the King and his Parliament the next day.

BUT …

I mean: "I was there!!"
Why is it that I can't find the words
to tell you about it?
I know I would be quite frightened if there was
say
a grizzly bear in the room, or a wolf
next to the window howling at the moon, as they do, I'm told,
head back, teeth snarling, or perhaps
a black widow spider silent on my desk
next to my hand.

This is worse, though, way more scary.

Look. My iPad is there,
the screen, an Olympic-sized pool
waiting for my dictated words to swim across it,
your cheers encouraging me to tell more,
and more. Keep going. Keep going.
The pens I bought last week, intending to write about my life,
still sealed in that plastic wrapping,
impossible to open with bare hands (or even gloved hands,
come to that),

The new journal, pages with squares

like a school exercise book
reminding me of days years ago in France,
in Paris and Normandy.
It has a black ribbon to mark the place
 where the most recently written paragraphs
should be telling you my story.   But ….

THERE (from Essex)

Looking across the river when it's clear
you can see the other side, a thin, dark line.
I must admit I've never been over there myself,
but I have heard stories.
There are some people, they say,
descendants of mermaids who came from France
in the 14th century, who still have webbed feet.
Others have eyes pale and grey as a January snowstorm
and wear sunglasses all the time, even in the rain.

It is said they pick up pizza with their fingers,

eating slices like savages, the cheese dripping.

They love ice cubes.
Their language is strange.
Their A is long, their O is strong and Scandinavian,
they don't use the letter T;
sometimes, a D - like warder instead of water,
Beddy for Betty,
other times a collection of stuttering syllables,
replacing the T or double T with a li'ul silent space.

On the other hand, it is frequently remarked,

the children are very polite,
hold doors open,
they say please and thank you,
and everything is very clean.

I THINK IT WAS TUESDAY EVENING

but it might have been Wednesday.
The days all seem the same recently; as I get old,
except Sunday,
when we have bacon sandwiches for breakfast,
and Thursday, which is trash day.
It must have been Tuesday, I realise,
because I had met Amy Rose at the airport,
coming home as she always does each year
to celebrate her birthday with us.

We waited in the driveway for a moment

after I closed the garage door.
The sun had set, but the sky in the west
still had colour.
There were the lights of a helicopter
 heading to somewhere in The Valley,
and one bright star just above the horizon.
I am told frequently, and I forget,
that stars twinkle, and planets are a solid light,
so, actually, it must have been a planet,
maybe Venus, setting.
The world seemed fresh and peaceful.
We stood and enjoyed it together.
before going into the house.

WOW!!! What was that?"
A bird had flown above our heads,
silently, gliding,
its wings, at least a yard across.
We felt the air disturbed,
like a gentle sneeze, and it was gone,

disappearing into one of Dan Saxon's trees
behind the wall of his garden opposite.

"It was The Owl," I whispered, "an omen perhaps,
a sign that your next year will be special."
After all, we are taught,
aren't we, to think of owls as wise and benevolent?
Often, I hear him, our owl, in the dark of early mornings
..."Who-whoo, who-whoo" ...
with perhaps a hint of a question,
calling to a friend higher up the hill,
who answers with what sounds to me exactly the same
..."who-whoo, who-whoo."
But I am not an expert on the calls of owls.

When I sit at breakfast with my Yorkshire tea
and brown toast with ginger jam or orange marmalade
reading The Guardian and The New York Times,
I sometimes call out, normally silently to myself
... "But-But-But. Why-Whyee?"
Quite definitely a question.I hear no answer.
I have to say, though, I am not an expert
on the speech of politicians.

APT

was the word that struck me.
I was riding backwards
looking at what we had already passed,
on the train to The North on the LNER,
traveling to a Writing Retreat.
Looking back, thinking of the past,
seemed just right.
I rode this same train when I was young,
at university, looking forward.
In those days the Flying Scotsman
left at 10, on the dot,
and the 4 o'clock to Leeds left at 4.00.
Now we are asked to admire and be impressed
by the efficiency of an 09.27 stopping at all stations
to Kings Lynn, or the 15.58 to Newcastle-upon-Tyne.
The doors today open with a button
and the lavatory is like a set from 'Startrek'.
That notice has gone … the wonderful statement,
"GENTLEMEN LIFT THE SEAT".
The smoke from the steam locomotive
which danced and swirled alongside the train
before dissolving into fields and trees …. GONE too.
But, looking back, I remember them.

WORDSDALE

It was raining all that week! Raining hard.
Words were literally pouring onto the pages of notebooks.
No drizzle here. No mist. This was a serious storm.
The County Council had even painted on the road outside,
in white letters 12-feet long, the word

S L O W

Take care, it suggested, you are entering

a THOUGHTZONE.

A place where, in the room where the clock ticked,

conversations were penned between inverted commas,

feelings were unfolded, opened, laid out in sentences,

characters stood in doorways between here and there,

Ideas were planted in plots to grow and bloom.
action moved at the speed of fingers,
scenes were seen, songs were sung,
mothers were remembered,
mysteries deepened, secrets spilled, or not,
ghosts walked through the walls of our minds,
and on Friday night we each unlocked the doors
of our private story gardens
and shared the beauty of what we had grown.
We discovered then
that what had been called a Retreat
for all of us had actually been Advance, a Victory.

The Garsdale Writers' Retreat, November 2022

I MUST ADMIT

Our snowman was pretty cool.
When the heat was on,
he simply melted

into his surroundings.

You could, though,
if you knew where to look,

make out a blue moth-eaten hat,

two pebbles, three red buttons,

and perhaps a carrot.

SPIDERS MAY BE CLOSER THAN THEY APPEAR

You're so vain.
You live inside a mirror
so that, in the evening or early morning,
when it is quiet, you can step outside
and watch yourself spinning webs,
admiring your long, slender legs
and the quality of the silk.

Your mirror ….
It's not an elegant or expensive address;
It's only a Toyota, after all, not an Audi, or a Porsche:
functional, one could say.
You travel to supermarkets and sit outside restaurants,
you have been to Pasadena, Hollywood, Glendale,
a thousand times,
and once, at over 60 miles an hour, to Disneyland,
the happiest place on earth.

Your nest inside the mirror is warm and dry,

and, by arachnic standards, quite comfortable;
Even the vibration could perhaps be considered exciting,
and you enjoy it, inside your mirror.

Inspidered by…

*the visitor who has lived in the
driver's side mirror of my wife
Dianne's Prius for months, surviving
the hot California sun, heavy
rainstorms, gale force winds, and
freeway driving.*

And Carly Simon: 'You're so Vain'

ELEANOR'S ASHESk

Words words words

the words. Where are they when we need them?

When we need to say we miss you.
We can talk amongst ourselves,

about incidents and events in our lives, of memories,

but it's not the same as when **you** told the stories,

your eyes smiling,
the stories of our childhood days,

of places you had been, of the people you had known.

No. It's not the same as when **you** told the stories

when we talk amongst ourselves.
Today, we bring your ashes here, to Laguna Beach,
your favourite place.
If we listen carefully, we can hear
the waves of the Pacific singing,
the surf and rocks and wind and sand
singing as quietly as our tears ….
      Welcome back, Eleanor.
      We have missed you.

(Words written for a friend, Laura, who sang them as she sprinkled her mother's ashes at Laguna Beach.)

I HAD MADE A BIG MISTAKE

Usually, on a long-distance flight, I take out my book as soon as I sit down. That way, it's unlikely that a conversation that could last for hours will begin.

Virgin Atlantic Airways flights leave from Terminal 3 at Heathrow, and it is a long, long walk from the check-in desk through Passport Control and Security to the departure lounge and then to the gate. I had put my book inside my carry-on suitcase to pull it along on wheels rather than carry it along the miles of moving walkways and hadn't remembered to take it out before I lifted the bag up into the overhead locker. I should have put it into my backpack with my Mars bar, Cadbury Fruit & Nut milk chocolate, the Maltesers, the cheese and cucumber sandwich my friend Kate had made for me in case the food was awful, and the paper bag with a quarter pound of Yorkshire Winter Mixture sweeties for me to suck while I read or watched a film. It would have been there next to my seat, but, no, because I had an exit row seat, I had to also put the backpack up there, too, and I didn't take out my book before I did that. Duh. No book to hide in.

My seat was in Premier Economy, the section with better seats and a glass glass for wine and food on a proper plate with a real knife and fork. Just 2 seats, window and aisle. I like the aisle these days, not being as supple as I used to be, finding it hard to squeeze and climb into and out of the window seat. In the window was a young woman in her late 20's, maybe.
I'd noticed her at the gate before boarding. Beautiful in an Orange County way, confident, athletic looking, remarkable strong blue eyes, blond hair in a ponytail, white t-shirt, denim jacket, ripped jeans, Apple things in her ears, expensive looking white soft shoes.

She was prepared. She had her book ready to read. Don't talk to me, it said. I saw it was 'The Six', the Laura Thompson book about the Mitford sisters, and I noticed she was way over halfway through it. It had been recommended to me at Skylight Books, my local bookshop, and I was tempted to ask about it, but the way she had immediately opened it after typing a last text before closing her phone sent that message quite clearly.

Don't talk to me.

After all, it's what I would have done if I had been prepared.

I wasn't. I sat just thinking for a while until the Fasten Seatbelt sign went out. I have recently become an expert at procrastination, a black belt, I maintain, so sitting thinking wasn't hard. Now I could stand up and lift down my backpack with my picnic supplies, my book, the latest Louise Penny Three Pines mystery, and the really comfortable and effective eye mask I had saved from the goody bag from an Upper-Class journey the year before.

Ten hours later …

THIS IS THE CAPTAIN SPEAKING

We are starting our descent now into Los Angeles.

We are due to arrive at 20.50, 8.50 pm local time.

Temperature there is currently 18, 65 Fahrenheit.

Thank you for flying with Virgin Atlantic.

On behalf of all the crew, I wish you a safe onward journey. Please prepare for landing.

The flight attendants were busy collecting rubbish, making

seatbacks upright, and for us in the Exit Row, taking our bags and putting them, "stowing them" they call it, up in the overhead bins.

"The Six" reader and I had both spent the journey sleeping and reading, and now here we were, almost there, flying over the glow of Los Angeles, the bright lines of the freeways, the arteries of the city: the 10, 210, 5, 55, the 710, the Harbor and the Hollywood Freeways, and then the 405 just feet below us as we swooped down to land at LAX.

She turned to me, smiled, and spoke:

You can see these lights from space, you know?

Mmm, I believe you.

Are you English? I heard you talking earlier. Are you visiting Los Angeles?

Haha. No, well, yes, ha, I used to be English, I suppose I still am, really, but actually, I have lived here for a long time, and I do have a U.S. passport. My wife is a Valley Girl, and she dragged me by the hair, screaming, about 40 years ago and I'm still here living in the Hollywood hills.

Listen at me, I don't like the idea of having a long conversation, and here I am telling her what my mother would have called the history of Adam's grandfather. I think I could have closed the chat there and then, but no. I kept it open.

And you? Are you from California?

No, no, I'm going home. My mother isn't well, and I need to visit.

Is she in LA? Do you have far to go?

Uhuh, quite a way.

111

Another flight, or is it a drive?

Her eyes smiled. They had that depth and intensity that teachers' eyes have. They look right into you. Grey blue.

Well, Both, really. I take a car to Santa Barbara, to Vandenberg Air Force Base and get a shuttle from there.

It was something about her accent that I couldn't quite place. Something. My wife says that her own accent, a Hollywood accent if there is such a thing, is the purest American, basing her theory on the fact that in the days when the majority of films and television shows were made in Los Angeles, the actors all had the same accent, and so it became the standard "American" just as in the old days the BBC had become the generic "British". Scots I know tell me that an Inverness or Elgin accent is the purist Scottish, and I am sure that there are Welsh and Irish, from the North and the Republic, who claim a particular local speech as their standard.

We British have fine-tuned our listening. We can immediately recognise Sloane Ranger (Chelsea aristocratic), Sandhurst (army officer), or Oxbridge (well-educated) and have a knack of placing a person in boxes of social status, education, and place of birth within a few sentences. Judgements are made quickly after listening to vocabulary, grammar, and regional pronunciation.

Maybe it was just that she was speaking fast like young women do. Listening to my daughters laughing and talking sometimes leaves me wondering ... are they speaking my language? Why can't I understand what they are saying? Same when they text, thumbs, both thumbs speeding over their screens like Olympic ice skaters. Myself I stumble along one finger at a time, deleting and correcting continually.

I wasn't afraid of getting involved in a long conversation ... we were close to landing ... so, politely, I answered.

Is your mother in the Air Force there? I guess her illness must be bad if you have flown home all this way.

Well, yes and no, she's with NASA, actually. She was an astronaut when I was born. And she had an accident last week and is in hospital.

Interesting: she had done it too. All that detail.

Oh dear. I'm sorry. You said you have to get a shuttle from Santa Barbara.

From Vandenberg, yes. My mother lives in the colony on the moon. I was born and grew up there.

The moon?

I know. It's a surprise, isn't it?

YES, IT IS, I thought.

She continued: *It's not technically a secret, but not many people know. There are about 5000 people living up there at the Luna Base. I went to school there before coming back to Earth to go to UC Berkeley. I live in London now.*

She smiled and laughed, a sweet little chuckle. Beautiful, perfect teeth and warm, kind eyes. We taxied into the gate. The engines went silent. There was that simultaneous seatbelt click as everyone stood up.

End of,
as they say in England.

Was she really a Luna Child, or a girl from Laguna Hills with a sense of humour?

THE WORLD

wouldn't be quite the same, would it,

if flowers were square
and leaves rectangular,

if cats could fly, and spiders

could sing,

or if the sea was always flat and still

and rivers flowed uphill?
But I know for sure, if it WAS true,
I would love you just the way I do.

LOOK UP

I started to paint daffodils today
but their cheerful laughing faces
couldn't hide the images of the Ukraine war
that have filled our lives this week.
The thousand people waiting for a train,
the hospital with broken windows,
the young woman who had lived five days in a cellar
and travelled three days to escape,
who told us:

"Please go outside,

look up and enjoy the sky."

I painted the daffodils for her.

What else can I do, but cry?

April 2022

DAFFODILS

THE POET

I have a friend who lives In Lincolnshire near Kings Lynn.
He is a poet, speaks poetry fluently,
comfortably translating ideas into flowers on a page.
Not the rhyming couplets of a medieval jester
his lines are avenues of thoughts planted carefully,
the leaves blowing and rustling as the eye passes them,
but with the branches solidly in place.
My own poems begin like jig saw puzzles,
usually in the dark,
too many pieces of sky that don't quite fit at first.
His pictures are complete as they arrive in his mind,
cobalt blue skies and perfect thatched roofs.
Like magic he can pluck a haiku from the air
without taking a breath.
Forests of words grow inside the rooms of his house.
The walls are shelved with the works of philosophers,
biographers, politicians, novelists, playwrights, scientists,
sociologists, even an old French paperback,
its pages neatly sliced, a copy of Madame Bovary.
He hears a concerto for cello or a string quartet
in the sound of the wind in trees,
a tractor passing on the lane next to the river, a fox barking,
the bats crying in the evening as they fly around the house.
He speaks poetry. He tastes poetry. He hears poetry.
He sees poetry. Windows for him are frames
for the watercolours he draws in his mind with a pen,
adding afterwards a splash of burnt umber or cadmium red.

My friend, Colin, is a poet.

MY FAVOURITE WINDOW

at my friend's house in Lincolnshire
when I visit

is the one halfway down the staircase
on the landing looking across the fields
and down into the garden.

It's a tall window.
so, it includes the sky all the way
until it touches the trees on the horizon.

On the lawn near the white bench
I see the ginger cat, still as a statue, hunting,
waiting for something,
anything really, to move;
a gnome in a grey hat standing
at the edge of the hedge seeing all, hearing all,
saying nothing, as gnomes do.

The window ledge is wide
(the walls of the old house are thick).
and has a collection
of bottles tall thin small round brown green,
I like to imagine a band, an orchestra,
its music reflecting the mood of the sky
at the beginning of the day …
gentle sonatas, fierce symphonies,
with added solos from the birds:
a blackbird or is it a thrush?
(I have lived away too long to hear the difference),
a chorus of a thousand chaffinches,
murders of crows balancing noisily
on swaying treetops nearby,
a robin robustly defending his empire …
This is my land, stay away,
a group of gulls passing by on their way inland
seeking one of those tractors with big wheels
ploughing dark soil in amazingly straight lines
guided algorithmically, they tell me,

by a satellite somewhere in the sky.
The driver, warm in his cab,
his coat behind him on a peg,
occasionally rolling a cigarette with tobacco
from a tin in his shirt pocket
held closed with a thick rubber band,
sipping coffee from a flask
he keeps in a cup holder right there, next to his hand,
singing the songs he learned at school
and from his grandmother
back in Lithuania.
Behind the tractor the gulls fight,
their battle a ballet of dancing wings and sharp beaks,
to win a worm or a beetle, perhaps a spider
suddenly made homeless by the sharp blades of the plough.

The window sees all this and
the bottle band plays
…here is another day.

In the evening though I imagine
just a low hum as I pass.
The window, dark now,
has the reflection of an old man
climbing the wooden hill to Bedfordshire,
as my mother used to say.

THE FRONT DOOR IS RARELY USED

There is a table just inside, a hall table, a small table,
just the right size to hold a bunch of keys,
a pair of gloves perhaps, sunglasses, maybe,
or the book brought in from the car.
In the shallow drawer a telephone directory,
Yellow Pages,from the year before last,
and (strangely) a Swiss Army knife.
Above it, a mirror on the wall,
intended as a stop on the way out,
possibly to check the angle of your hat,
or make sure there are no egg-stained crumbs
in your beard,
a possible embarrassment when asking for a small Hovis
and two Eccles cakes at the bread shop in the town.
On the other side, a so-called Hall Stand,
hooks buried under several heavy coats
to be worn with Wellington boots
on cold, wet winter walks along the fen.
A ceramic elephant foot holds umbrellas;
the one, a gift from the Mercedes dealership,
that blew inside out the first time it was used,
a small individual version
with a button to launch its black sails
that doesn't work unless you know
exactly *how* to press it,the old boring black one
that pinches fingers enough to bleed when being closed,
kept as a family heirloom,
a reminder of the days in the 1950s
when a bowler hat and a tightly rolled brolly

were the uniform worn on commuter trains
from Woking, West Byfleet, Worplesdon,
Walton-on-Thames, and Weybridge,
from Essex, Sussex, Berkshire, St Albans, and the Chilterns
into Waterloo, Paddington, Victoria, Charing Cross,
and all the other city termini,
always, of course, with a briefcase to carry lunch
…an apple or a tangerine, a fish paste sandwich,
and a bag of crisps.

The door is firmly closed,
secured by two enormous bolts, top and bottom
and a huge ancient black lock, dating back possibly
to the days of Oliver Cromwell
and the Civil War, with a key
so large it would never fit in a pocket.
Above it at eye level a dainty gold Yale lock,
never used though because the key was lost years ago.
The door has a large window with colored leaded glass panes,
diamonds and squares, mostly bright red,
blue, and green, but because the window
faces north and has no sun
the colours spilling across the black and white tiled floor
are pale.

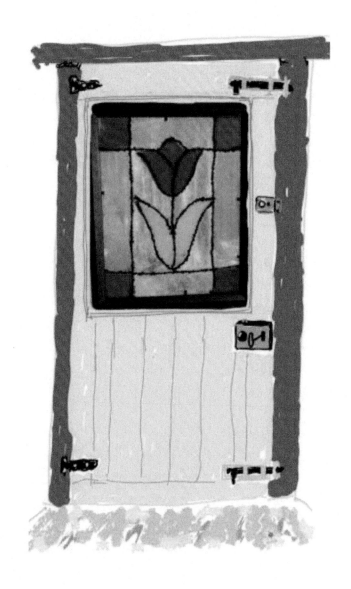

ROUNDHAY PARK, LEEDS, February

There had been a storm at the coast, I heard,
so when I drove through the park this morning,
I wasn't surprised to see it full of birds,
a gathering of gulls visiting, sitting on the grass,
like a picnic, a convention, a meeting, a festival,
a rally.
Kittiwakes sleeping on a flooded football field.
Lesser Black Backs -- packed into penalty areas --
defending their mud.
Plovers fidgeting prettily on sidelines.
One large bird, perched on the crossbar of the goal,
seemed to be addressing the members
of the gathering of feathered seaside brethren ......
"Brothers and sisters,
welcome. Sadly, I have to tell you that
sitting ducks and even swans
have been beaten up at the boating lake
by gangs of hungry herring gulls.
Small children,
their paper bags filled with stale scones
and dry crusts of whole-wheat bread,
have been terrified."

Motions were passed.

A LADY HIPPOPOTAMUS

I once knew
at the zoo
could open her mouth so wide
about twenty-two
small children could easily walk inside
and touch her epiglotamus.

About The Author

THE POET

 He lives in California but spells glamour with a 'U' and pronounces water and better with a 'T'. Sandeman Craik, also known as Jim, was born, grew up, and lived in England until moving to LA in 1984. He had spent two years National service in the army before training at Leeds University to teach. He spent his working life teaching and in the tourist industry as a tour guide in Britain, Europe, and Southern California.

Immerse yourself in the captivating world of this talented wordsmith, an artist whose life unfolds on the pages of this book. With a seamless blend of poignant poems and evocative illustrations, he invites readers on a journey through the highs and lows of human experience. He shares reflections on love, loss, and the tapestry of existence, making each piece a poignant exploration of the soul. This collection is more than a book, it's a testament to a life well lived and the celebration of the enduring power of creativity. Open these pages and discover the profound beauty that emerges when words and art intertwine with the essence of one man's remarkable journey.

Printed in Great Britain
by Amazon

36540999R00076